Act Normal

And Don't Tell Anyone About

The Castle Made Of Sweets

By Christian Darkin

First Printing 2016 by Rational Stories

www.RationalStories.com

The illustrations are by the author but use some elements for which thanks and credits go to www.obsidiandawn.com, kuschelirmel- stock, Theshelfs and waywardgal at Deviantart.com
Story and illustrations by © Christian Darkin.

CHAPTER 1

You may have already heard a story about a house made of sweets before. That is a fairy story and it has a witch and some children who get lost in a wood.

This is not that story. I don't like fairy stories. Fairy stories have castles and dragons in them, and they have damsels in distress.

A damsel is a girl, and distress is a special kind of trouble where you don't do anything to help yourself, you just sit and wait for somebody else to come and rescue you.

This story has a sort of castle in it, and a sort of dragon, and I am a girl, so I suppose I am a sort of damsel. I am also in trouble a lot, but I am NEVER in distress...

People in this story:

Me: I am Jenny. When I see something that makes me upset, I do something about it. I am not really old enough for grown-ups to listen to me to start with. But once I start doing things they usually have to listen because if they don't, the trouble just gets bigger and bigger.

Adam: My little brother, Adam can do lots of things well. He can hide really well, and he can shout really loud. These things are sometimes good and sometimes bad. He can shout so loud that people often say, "I can't hear myself think!" That means he has shouted so hard he has got into their brains and stopped the brain cells talking to each other.

Dad: Dad helps us when things get really bad. He tries not to help us too much. He likes it when we, "Sort it out between ourselves," because that is good practice for being older. Sometimes, he does have to help - like when there are dinosaurs or robots, or when there are too many real live rhinos in the house.

CHAPTER 2

Sometimes, my brother, Adam and I get to walk home from school with our friend Alfred who is a bit older. When we do, we get sweets, and then we go to play in the castle.

There is a thing I find very odd about sweets. Every kind of pack of sweets and every kind of box of chocolates, and every kind of bag of pick-and-mix has the same very odd thing about it:

There are always lots of nice sweets, and a few Ok sweets, but there is always one kind of sweet in the pack or the box or the bag that nobody likes at all.

I got whizzy fizzers – and the purple ones just taste like dust made of soap.

My brother, Adam got monster chews and the green ones with the wiggly legs are SO chewy that you can't ever get them off your teeth. If you eat one, your food tastes of green monster chew for 3 days even if you brush your teeth with a brush for cleaning shoes or toilets!

Alfred got hard sucky sweets and they have a blue one which you can stamp and stamp and stamp and it never breaks. When you suck it for a really long time then bite it really hard, it does break into sharp little bits that cut your gums and the inside tastes of coffee. Anyway, like always, we got them and went to the castle to play.

It's not really a castle. It is an old church with gaps in the walls, but we call it a castle. The grown-ups call it a dangerous structure – which is what they call things when they don't want kids to play in them.

It can't be very dangerous because it is very, very old and it is still standing up OK, and has only fallen down a little bit.

The tower is still high, and you can still climb up it and look out over the town. It feels like you are in a real castle.

I went up there to think about my plans (I have a lot of plans) and draw pictures.

Alfred and Adam played a fighting, shouting game up and down the tower. I think they were being baddies or monsters. Adam did some hiding, and he is very good at it.

Dad has a way to find him when he hides, but Dad wasn't there, so we had to wait for Adam to come out.

When they had finished, we all sat at the top and ate our sweets. At the end, all we had left were the purple whizzy fizzers, the green monster chews and the hard blue sweets.

Then we did what we always do with them. We pushed them into the little gaps in the walls of the castle. There must be a space behind the wall because you can hear them rattling down the inside of the walls sometimes when you push them in.

We love the castle. All the kids in the town love the castle. There are always people here playing, and eating sweets, and everyone has a sweet that nobody likes that gets pushed through the gaps into the space between the walls.

I think the bad sweets can't be a mistake because there is one in every single pack of sweets. I think they must be tests.

I think the people who make the sweets must test out ideas for making pillows and car wheels and bombs and spaceships and when they don't work, they use the bits up in sweets.

I do a lot of tests and when my tests don't work, I just use them for something else, so I think that must be what happens.

When we had finished our sweets, we went home, but the next day at school, we found out the worst bit of news ever...

CHAPTER 3

Mr. Grey came to talk to the school from the council. We had seen Mr. Grey before. When strange things happen in our town, he usually comes to the school, and tries to fix them.

When he gets here, I am usually fixing them myself, so I have to act normal so that he doesn't stop me. When he tries to fix them, it usually makes things worse (like when I made the ice-cap in the library. He made that A LOT worse).

He is sort of my enemy.

He looks very old and usually he is frowning. Today he was happy.

"Good news!" he said to the school, "We are going to pull down the old church because it is a dangerous structure, and build a big block there instead. It will improve the town."

The word, IMPROVE is supposed to mean making things better. This is why Mr. Grey is my enemy. He says things as if they're good even when they're bad.

He had a big table with a cloth over it. When he pulled the cloth away, we saw what he was so happy about. It was a model of our castle. Next to it were some little models of yellow diggers and little workmen in orange coats.

Next to that was another model. It was a model of what he wanted to put there instead. It was a big, grey box with little grey windows. There were no places to hide or climb and there were no gaps in the walls. There were no weeds or rocks or anything growing in it.

"We are very happy because the plans for the building have already won a prize," said Mr. Grey.

We all went up to look at the model. Adam liked the diggers. Then he used one to knock down the big grey box. Then he started pushing it around the hall.

Mr. Grey started to chase him. Everyone was laughing. Adam crashed through the curtain and behind the stage. Nobody could find him.

Adam is very good at hiding, but I could see where he had gone. I just managed to catch him before Mr. Grey did.

"Give the digger back," I said.

Adam laughed and gave it to me. I gave it back to Mr. Grey.

He said, "I hope you're not going to make trouble, young lady," which was not nice because I had got his digger back for him.

I said, "No, Mr. Grey. I'm just going to stop you."

At lunch in the library, I looked up the plans on the Internet. They had won a prize. It was a prize for being the most boring, rubbish building plans for that whole year.

I also looked up how to save our castle.

The Internet said there was a list of buildings which were not allowed to be pulled down. To get on that list, our castle would have to be very old and very special and it would have to be not like any other building in the world.

Our castle didn't count. Really it was just a falling down bit of an old church.

The Internet did say that sometimes if people all got together and had a meeting, they could think of clever plans to stop things being pulled down.

That's when I decided to have a meeting...

CHAPTER 4

I told everyone in the playground, that we were all going to meet at the castle on the way home.

Lots of people came to the meeting. The castle was full of children and we all had sweets to keep us going. I wanted to talk to them, but they were all very loud and they were all talking about the castle being pulled down so nobody could hear me.

I used Adam to make them quiet. Adam stood up at the very top of the castle and shouted really loud for a really long time.

When Adam shouts, you have to listen to him because he is so loud that you cannot hear yourself think. He once shouted even louder than a rocket taking off – but that is in another story.

Adam also does not stop shouting until everyone listens to him, so very soon everyone was quiet. He was also doing a dance, so they all looked at him too.

when he stopped, I stood up and said, "This is OUR castle. Do you want to save our castle?"

Everyone shouted, "YES!"

This is a trick I learned from Mr. Grey. If you ask people a question when you already know the answer is, "Yes," then they will get used to saying, "Yes." Then they will say, "Yes," to everything else even if they thought they were going to say, "No," before.

I use that trick on my brother a lot.

I said, "Will everyone do what I say?"

Everyone shouted, "YES!" (You see, it works!)

Then I said, "Everybody get your rubbish sweets," everyone knew I meant the sweets they didn't like, "and stick them to the castle walls."

Everyone did. The whole school took all their hardest toffees and their most tooth breaking boiled sweets, and their chewiest chews and their stringiest, stretchiest stringy sweets and their dustiest fizzes and their gloopiest gummy sweets, and they glued them to the walls.

And everyone poured the stickiest sludgy bits from the bottoms of their slushy drinks down the sides of the walls.

They did this until the whole wall was covered in shiny rainbow coloured sweets and they looked like the best collage in the world.

It looked like the castle was really MADE of sweets!

I said, "Now everyone who sees the castle will know that this is not an empty place or a place that nobody goes. This is our place. It is our castle made of sweets, and we will defend it!"

Everyone cheered because I got louder and louder towards the end of what I was saying – and that was another thing I learned from Mr. Grey. If you do that then everyone knows they have to cheer at the end.

But I knew Mr. Grey would still pull the castle down. We needed more ideas, so I said, "Get into groups and think of plans to stop them pulling down our castle. Draw your plans on a piece of paper."

Everyone got into groups, and I started going from one group to the next looking at what they were drawing.

Alison and some of her friends were first. They had drawn lots of flowers.

"What is your plan?" I asked.

"We should plant a big garden around the castle," Alison said, "If it looks really lovely, they won't want to run over the flowers."

I didn't think that would stop them.

Alison said, "Some of the plants will be nettles and some will have thorns – like in Sleeping Beauty."

Nicola added, "-and we will have a sign which will say 'keep off the grass'."

I said, "A garden will take too long to grow."

Then I looked at Alfred's friends plan. They had done lots of drawings. I could see some people running but they were on fire and there was a big scribbly cloud.

I said, "What is your plan?"

Alfred said, "Zombie robots!"

I said, "I'm not sure we can make zombie robots."

Alfred said, "But you made them before".

That was true, but it was weeks ago and it is in another story. Anyway, I made them by mistake and I have found that zombie robots tend to make more problems than they fix.

There were a lot of other plans too.

A lot of people planned to write letters. Also, lots of people planned to have a demonstration — which is when people all get together and stand in front of the diggers and sometimes they make a kind of wall with boxes to stop the diggers.

I didn't think that would work because if they could pull down a castle, they could probably pull down the boxes too.

Some people had other ideas with lasers and tanks and a charity song.

A team from class 2c had a plan I didn't really understand, but it had squirrels in it and they were driving toy cars.

I was just going to ask them what it was about, but I didn't get the chance because there was a big noise outside the castle.

It was a little bit like the noise a herd of elephants would make if they were trampling through a competition to find out who had the loudest hoover.

The noise made the whole castle shake and bits of brick and a few sweets fell off the walls. Everybody stopped drawing and talking and we all went outside.

That was when we saw what had made the noise, and it was very bad.

Mr. Grey's diggers had arrived...

CHAPTER 5

There were 5 diggers. They were very big, and very yellow. Their tracks were as tall as me, and each one had a big cab with lights that looked like eyes which shone in our faces.

The noise was really, really loud and the big, metal machines shook with the sound of their engines and smoke came out of big chimneys on their tops.

The one at the front was the biggest. It had a wide, scoop which was big enough for my whole class to climb inside and get lifted up. I was a bit scared because of the noise and because they were all so big.

Adam wasn't scared. Adam doesn't know how to be scared yet, and he loves big machines. He likes diggers best of all. Diggers and tanks. And big trains. And he likes trucks and helicopters and ships. And tunnel drilling machines. He really likes all big machines, but diggers are best for him because they break things and he loves breaking things.

I saw Adam run around behind one of the diggers, but I couldn't follow him because then I saw Mr. Grey.

Mr. Grey stood in front of the biggest digger. He had a yellow hard hat on and a plan on a big piece of paper. He also had a loudhailer which he spoke into. It made his voice loud and boomy.

He said, "This is a dangerous structure. Everybody must go home! Tomorrow we will pull this building down!"

I said, "You cannot pull it down because we don't want you to."

He said, "I can!" and he pointed at his plans.

Then I pointed at all our plans. We had lots more plans than he had. Ours were much better than his too - They had flowers and squirrels driving toy cars and even some robot zombies.

But Mr. Grey didn't think our plans were better. He went into the castle. He got all our plans together in a big heap on the floor.

Then while we all watched, Mr. Grey got a match and set fire to all our plans.

That was very bad. You are not supposed to set fires inside a building.

I told him, but he said that it didn't matter because he was going to pull the building down in the morning anyway.

While he was telling me that, Adam ran up behind him, grabbed his plans and threw them on the fire. Then he ran back behind the machines.

We all laughed, but he said that it didn't matter because they were only copies and that he could make a hundred copies if he wanted. I knew he was right because the plans were on the Internet, and you can't burn the Internet.

"Now, get out, all of you!" he shouted through his loudhailer (he didn't even need to use it. The machines were switched off and it was all quiet).

All his men got together and started chasing us away from the castle. Everyone started running around and soon we were all outside being chased away.

I went up to Mr. Grey, and said, "Don't you see - this is the children's place? This is our castle. Weren't you ever a child?"

He just looked at me and through his loudhailer, he shouted, "Get out!"

I think if Mr. Grey ever was a child, he has forgotten what it's like.

I was so angry that I just stomped all the way home, and it wasn't until I got to the door that I noticed Adam wasn't with me...

CHAPTER 6

As soon as he saw I was on my own, Dad grabbed his coat and we started running back to the castle to find my brother. It wasn't far, but Dad says we must ALWAYS stay together, ESPECIALLY when strange things are happening.

On the way, I told Dad everything that had happened. I told him about the castle made of sweets, and I told him that Mr. Grey was going to pull it down in the morning. And I told him about the meeting and all the plans we had made, and how Mr. Grey had burnt them INDOORS.

Dad said that was the wrong thing for him to have done.

When we got to the castle, Mr. Grey and his men had all gone home to wait for morning. The diggers were all switched off and empty.

Adam is very good at hiding, and once he hid for a whole afternoon inside a bathroom cabinet. But Dad has a special way of finding him that always works.

Dad walked up to one of the diggers. He stuck his tongue out and made a loud farting noise. Nothing happened – which meant that Adam was not there.

Then he went up to the next digger and made a farting noise again. We listened, but nothing happened.

Then he went up to the biggest digger of all, and he made a really loud farting noise that wobbled and splattered all over the place.

From inside the digger's scoop came a little snuffling sound, then a giggle, then a loud laugh. The laugh didn't stop, it just kept getting louder and louder. In the end, Adam fell out of the scoop, rolling around in the mud, laughing and giggling at the noise Dad had made.

Adam ALWAYS laughs when Dad makes farting noises, and the more he tries to be quiet and hide, the more he laughs and giggles. That is Dad's special way of finding Adam when he hides.

"Come on," said Dad, "It's time to go home and have tea," but then he stopped, and he looked up at the castle in a kind of sad way.

"What's the matter?" I said.

Dad said, "I remember this place." He walked in through the broken bit of castle where all our sweets were stuck to the wall. He said, "I used to play here when I was little. Granny said she used to play here too. Are they really pulling it down?"

I said, "Yes. Tomorrow."

Adam said, "No, they're not."

Dad looked at the sweets stuck to the walls, "We used to eat our fruit gums here," he said, "and our candy twists - except the pink ones. You could never crunch the pink ones."

"They're not going to pull it down tomorrow," said Adam.

Dad said, "We used to push the pink ones through the gaps in the bricks, and you could hear them rattling down the insides of the walls," he said, "It sounds silly, doesn't it?"

I said, "No, we do the same thing with the sweets we can't eat."

Dad wasn't listening. He was just looking up at the castle walls and remembering being a kid. Adam pulled my shirt and said, "They're not going to pull it down. Shall I show you why?"

Adam took me outside to where the big machines were, and he showed me what he'd been doing while he'd been hiding.

I didn't tell Dad...

CHAPTER 7

The next morning, we all went back to the castle. Everyone was there. All the children from school were standing around sadly watching. Mr. Grey and his men were getting into their machines and getting ready to do their work. All the grown-ups were there too, all lined up around the outside of the castle, watching.

The whole town had come to watch the old broken building finally being pulled down.

Mr. Grey stepped forward.

He looked as if he was about to make a speech, but then his men started their diggers, and the great, loud roaring sound of 5 huge diggers filled the air.

The town held its breath. Adam started to giggle. Mr. Grey pointed at the big machine at the front, and waved at it. The great, huge scoop which could fit my whole class in rose up into the air in front of the castle. Adam started hopping around from one foot to the other, grinning.

Mr. Grey waved the digger forward ready to smash into the side of our castle. Its engine got louder and louder.

Then suddenly, BOING! The moment the digger started to move forward, there was a snapping, grinding sound from deep inside the machine's engine. Orange smoke started pouring out. Then the smoke turned green, then blue, then red.

There was a smell like burnt sugar, and broken metal and blueberries all mixed together. The big digger shook and spluttered and then, its engine stopped. The great scoop came crashing down. There was silence.

One by one, Mr. Grey ordered the other machines forward and one by one, they juddered and snapped and broke down, pouring rainbow coloured smoke into the sky, and smelling like candy on fire.

Mr. Grey did not know what had happened. He ran up to the biggest digger, and flung open its engine cover. The smoke slowly blew away.

Underneath, the whole of the inside of the engine was filled with broken and melted bits of sweets.

That was what Adam had been doing while he was hiding. That was what he had showed me while Dad was looking up at the castle and remembering being a child.

Adam had got some of the sticky, crunchy sweets from the wall of the castle, and stuck them into the diggers' engines. When the men had started their machines, the sweets had broken and melted and jammed into the engines, and the diggers had broken down.

Adam was jumping around by now, laughing and giggling. Adam loves it when things break, and he thought he had saved the castle.

Some of the children started to clap. Mr. Grey was angry. His face started to turn red, and he shouted at his men. But we soon found out that he was not finished yet...

CHAPTER 8

Mr. Grey pulled out a phone and started talking into it. He was calling for help.

In a few minutes, his help arrived. Around the corner came what looked like a great metal dragon, taller than all the houses. Its body was wide and flat and low, and it rolled along on two huge sets of tracks. Each track was taller than Dad and wide enough to squash our car. The dragon's tail was a crane and on the end was a huge heavy ball. Its neck was a long arm rising out of the front with a steel head like a jaw big enough and high enough to grab the chimney from a house and crush it into powder.

I knew that if I was going to save the castle, I would have to beat the dragon, but I didn't know how.

The dragon slowly chugged up to the castle. Then, it drove around the castle in a big circle. Its driver looked up and down the building trying to work out which bit to knock down first.

The tracks were so big and the dragon was so heavy that it dug a deep hole like a moat all around the castle with its tracks.

Then it stopped at the wall of the tower, and turned so that the great ball was swinging in front of the castle. The crane swung back and then forward and the ball swung into the tower.

CRASH!!

There was no way the castle could take it, and I saw the wall starting to wobble, then topple, and a great cloud of smoke rose up as the bricks crashed to the ground and crumbled into powder.

The dragon had won. With one smash of its tail, the stone walls had fallen down. The town gasped.

But when the smoke cleared, we all saw that something amazing had happened...

CHAPTER 9

The ball had broken all the walls. The bricks had crumbled into a big pile of dust, but what was between the walls hadn't fallen.

And what was between the walls?

Sweets!

Thousands and thousands of sweets of every colour. Monster chews that were too chewy and whizzy fizzers that were like rock dust and blue sucky sweets that would never break.

The hardest of hard candies, the stringiest of stretchy sweets and the gummiest of gummy drops. Gobstoppers that would never melt and gum that had been chewed and chewed until it couldn't be chewed any more.

The thrown away sweets of a thousand children over a hundred years all rattling down the inside of the walls, and sticking together into a gloopy colourful mess getting stronger and harder and higher every time a new set of children found the castle and dropped their new kinds of sweets into the biggest pick and mix in the world.

At the top of the tower, I could see all our old sweets sitting in a thin layer. Lower down must have been Dad's old sweets and granny's and maybe even more before her.

Today's sweets and last year's sweets and sweets from a hundred years ago with names nobody even remembers, squashed and melted together into the walls of our castle.

Mr. Grey looked up at the coloured walls, and he ordered the dragon on. The great ball of its tail swung again, but it hit a wall of jelly sweets and it just bounced off.

It swung again, and hit a wall of chewy gum. It just made a sort of squelchy dent which did no harm.

It swung back and gave a great big crash into a wall of hard boiled sweets. The ground shook. At the bottom where the dragon's tracks had dug out a moat around the castle, I saw a little trickle of something blue and gooey flowing out from under the walls.

I looked back to the dragon. The great ball cracked like a giant conker, and fell to the ground.

Mr. Grey ordered the dragon to turn around. Now its jaw was facing the castle. The head moved up and down.

I knew the castle couldn't stand up if that scoop started eating away at it! But I had just thought of a plan...
I grabbed Adam and we ran past the dragon and into the hole its wheels had made around the castle. The blue gooey stuff was dribbling out of a door in the ground at the bottom of the castle.

We all knew about the door. It used to lead into a crypt under the old church, but none of us had ever been able to open it. Now, I knew why.

All the sloppiest and gloopiest and gooiest sweets from the last hundred years must have dripped and flowed slowly down into the crypt through the walls.

The doors were stuck fast in all that sweet goo. But now the ball hitting the walls had opened the door a bit.

Adam and I grabbed the door and pulled hard. It cracked. We pulled again even harder and it moved. We pulled a third time and just as the dragon's great head was about to bite down on the castle walls, the door flew open and out poured a sea of sticky gluey sweet mix.

The blue goo flowed into the moat, over the dragon's tracks and up into its engine. And it kept flowing. The moat filled, the dragon was pulled along by the river of sticky sugar until the driver leapt out and it tipped and sank into the blue slime.

That's when the strangest thing happened...

CHAPTER 10

I looked over at Mr. Grey. I thought he'd be angry, but he wasn't.

He was just standing at the bottom of the castle wall. Slowly, he reached out his hand and touched a little patch of sweets.

"Cola gums..." he said quietly, "I put these here, a long time ago," and now suddenly, Mr. Grey didn't look old anymore. And he didn't look scary.

He just looked like a little boy playing where he shouldn't have been playing with a bag of sticky sweets he couldn't eat.

And then the whole town started pointing. Everyone remembered the times they'd played at the castle and everyone looked for the old sweets they'd thrown away all those years ago.

Dad found his flying saucers that he said tasted of cardboard, and Mrs. Brant found her honey nuggets that covered your teeth. A policeman found space-dust that crackled on your tongue and the dragon's driver found a whole tangle of sticks of rock he'd brought home from a holiday but never been able to eat.

I was still a bit worried that they might want to pull our castle down in the end. But do you remember that list I'd found on the Internet of buildings nobody was allowed to pull down?

Well, two weeks later, our castle made of sweets was put on that list. It turned out that it was very old, and it was very special, and it was not like any other building in the world.

And that's how a damsel who was never in distress beat a dragon and saved a secret castle that nobody knew about, but everybody built.

And there wasn't even a knight in shining armour, unless you count Adam, which I think I do.

The end.

Act Normal and read more...

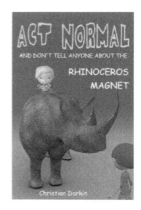

Made in the USA
Middletown, DE
16 October 2021